THE RANSOM NOTE

THE RANSOM NOTE

J. M. GOODSPEED

ILLUSTRATED BY
RAY KEANE

Xerox Education Publications

Publishing, Executive and Editorial Offices:
Xerox Education Publications
Middletown, Connecticut 06457

ISBN 0-88375-216-6

Library of Congress Catalogue Card Number: 78-51340

Weekly Reader Children's Book Club edition

Weekly Reader Book Division offers book clubs for
children from preschool to young adulthood. All
quality hardcover books are selected by a distinguished
Weekly Reader Selection Board.

For further information write to:
Weekly Reader Book Division
1250 Fairwood Avenue
Columbus, Ohio 43216

for Fred

The ransom note came on Saturday morning.

Liz couldn't believe it. Someone had really kidnapped Nelly.

"Anyone who would kidnap a poor, defenseless little dog has got to be a monster." Liz walked quickly to the sink with her breakfast dishes. Her long, thin legs made her the tallest girl in her sixth grade class. She always moved quickly, almost with a glide.

"Do you think Sam will pay the ransom?" Jake asked.

"Certainly, silly. As soon as she finds out how much they want. You know how she loves Nelly. She'd probably sell her house if she had to."

"What if we could rescue Nelly ourselves?" Jake

1

jumped up from the table, knocking the milk carton over. Liz just managed to reach over and grab it in time. With a look of annoyance she tossed her long hair and put her hands on her hips.

"Where do you think you'd look that Sam hasn't already tried? Anyway, whoever took her must have her hidden, but good."

"I know, and Nelly just loves everyone, even strangers. Maybe we could just snoop around town and we might hear her barking."

"Supposing she's been tranquilized? You know, drugged. Then where are you?" asked Liz smugly.

"Well, it's better than just sitting here waiting for the phone to ring. Aunt Sam'll sit by it all day, so she can pay the ransom for Nelly."

"I thought you were going to the park to play ball. Don't tell me you'd give that up!" said Liz.

"Sure—for Sam and Nelly I would," said Jake. "I'd even leave my skateboard home."

"I'm supposed to meet Janet this afternoon. We're planning the school picnic next month."

"Well, can't you do that later? Nelly is more important."

"You're right," said Liz. "I'll call Janet right now."

Jake rinsed his cereal bowl and put it in the dishwasher. He knew if he didn't Liz would yell at him. It wasn't easy having a sister two grades ahead of you and over three inches taller. But what Jake lacked in inches he made up for in motion, his mother always said.

He grabbed his baseball cap and planted it squarely on his head. As Liz came back from the phone, he said, "Let's go next door and snoop around at Sam's. Maybe we can find a clue."

Liz took off her gold-rimmed glasses and carefully washed them under the tap. She dried them on the towel, wondering how she always got them so bent. Someday, she hoped soon, she'd get a chance to have contact lenses. As long as she had to wear glasses forever she wanted to try them. When she put the big round rims back on, they gave her long, thin face an owlish look. Then she slid into her clogs, which really made her tower over Jake.

She followed him out the back door and they crossed the lawn in silence. Liz found herself automatically looking around the ground as she walked. Her glasses slid down, and she wrinkled her nose to keep them up. She felt silly because she had no idea what she was looking for.

"Here's the hole by the fence Nelly uses to get out of the yard. Sam can never figure out how she gets loose." Jake grinned, remembering the day he had hidden on the other side of the fence, watching Nelly pull her disappearing act.

The hole behind the back of the garage was also

Nelly's secret hiding place when she knew she'd be punished for eating the tulip tops or chewing on the back step rug.

Jake pushed aside the bushes and bent down and felt in the hole. His eyes flew open. He drew his hand out holding a long, thin whistle.

"What's that?" asked Liz, squatting down beside him.

Jake blew on the thing and nothing came out. "It's just an old whistle that doesn't work," he said.

"Let me see." Liz grabbed the whistle and blew. Again, the air just rushed through it. "Jake, this *is* a clue! It's an animal whistle. I saw one on TV. Dogs can hear it, but we can't."

She jumped up and started for Aunt Sam's house. "Where are you going?" yelled Jake as he ran to keep up with her.

"I want to find out if Sam ever had one of these. I don't think she did. You know what? The kidnapper could have used it to call Nelly."

"But how did it get in her hole?"

"How do I know? But if it belonged to the kidnapper, it's a clue."

She ran through the back door yelling, "Sam, Sam! Are you here?"

"Of course. I'm upstairs trying to be calm. Come on up." The shout came from Sam's studio.

Some people thought their Aunt Samantha was a bit odd. She wore old jeans covered with paint spots and dried clay. If anyone called her Samantha to her face, she was likely to toss a paint brush or a clump of clay at them. She'd answer only to Sam. Liz was very proud of her Aunt Sam. Her sculptures and pottery were in many of the biggest museums, so Liz thought Sam had a right to be called any name she wanted.

"You wait here," Liz said to Jake. She took the narrow stairs two at a time and barged into the studio room. Sunlight streamed in from the big windows, which were a large part of the high, painted roof. Sam was bent over her work table, throwing a big blob of gray clay on the surface. Then she pounded it fiercely with her fist.

"I'm working off some of my anger and fears," she said between gritted teeth.

"Did you call the police?" asked Liz.

"No, not yet. The note said not to, and I'm so afraid they'll kill the little thing."

"Kill her! No one could possibly kill Nelly," squawked Liz.

"Honey, there are thousands of dog-nappings every year. People either resell the dog if they can get enough money, or ..." Sam's voice cracked and she threw the clay down with a bang.

"Or what?" asked Liz cautiously.

"Or they sell them for laboratory experiments, or kill them." Sam's voice took a high pitch and reached the top of the two-story ceiling.

"Oh, Sam!" cried Liz. "We've got to find her. Please call the police."

"I will if the kidnappers haven't called me by noon. I just thought ..." She faltered, then went on, "I just thought they might return her safely if they thought I'd pay for her."

We've got to find her, thought Liz. We can't let Nelly die.

Liz moved over to the long work table and picked up a small lump of damp clay. She looked at Sam's thin, bony face. There were streaks on it from the clay dust and beads of perspiration running down her forehead. Liz thought some of the streaks might have been made by a tear or two.

Liz dropped the clay, rubbed her hands on the seat of her jeans and turned to Sam.

"Did you ever have a dog whistle for Nelly?" Liz asked, trying to keep the excitement out of her voice.

"Of course not!" Sam answered. "Nelly doesn't think she's a dog. She'd never have paid any attention to one of those things. Why?" She stopped pounding long enough to look up at Liz.

"Oh, nothing, really. I just thought it might help to whistle for her." She smiled lamely.

"Nonsense. She's a prisoner. That's what the note said. They'll get whatever they ask for, but my Nelly better be safe." She picked up the clay and slammed it down again. The water on the board splattered all over her shirt. Wisps of dark hair that had escaped from her pony tail fell across her forehead.

"Oh, I'm sure she'll be okay." Liz assured her. She started backing out of the room.

"What's your hurry?" Sam asked.

"I've got to run ... an errand. I'll be back later to see if you've heard any more."

Liz bolted down the stairs, almost landing on top of Jake sprawled on the bottom step. "Come on, quick," she whispered.

Once they were outside Liz started to clomp toward the center of town. "Where are we going?" Jake yelled in her ear.

"Pet shop, silly. Find out who owns a dog whistle."

"Hey, what if a lot of people do?" He stopped short at the corner.

"Jake, we've got to try. It's our only clue and we've got to find Nelly. Sam's so upset."

"Okay, but it's probably a wild goose chase," he answered.

"You're the one who started this, so let's go," she replied.

They crossed the main street and went right straight

to the little store next to the big gift and card shop. The Animal House was run by Mr. Goodman. Liz and Jake had given him a lot of business in gerbils and hamsters in the past. They were between pets now and were desperately trying to convince their mother that they were old enough and responsible enough to take care of a dog.

The bell tinkled as they entered the shop, and Mr. Goodman came from the back bird cages. Liz thought he looked a bit like a parrot himself.

"Good morning. How are you two this sunny day?"

"Fine, Mr. Goodman."

Liz and Jake moved around the tiny shop, looking at

the rabbits, gerbils and a litter of kittens in the store window. In spite of all the animals, the smell was clean, almost sterile. Liz petted one of the kittens behind the ear, then turned to Mr. Goodman.

"We're interested in those silent dog whistles. You know, the ones people can't hear."

"You have a new puppy?" he asked, beaming.

"No, no it's not exactly that we want to buy one. It's more like we want to know who has already bought one from you."

"You want to borrow one?" he asked with surprise.

"No, we want to return one," Liz said in a rush.

Jake looked at her with fury as if she were about to give away their clue right then.

"We found one and we thought you might know whose it is," she continued.

Mr. Goodman shook his head. "I've sold so many of them," he said. "As a matter of fact, I'm all sold out." He turned and pointed at an empty rack. "I thought I had one left, but someone must have bought it and I didn't realize it."

"Where's Stanley? Maybe he'd know who bought it," asked Jake.

"He's at home. He's never here in the shop," he answered. "Why don't you go by and see him?"

"Maybe, if we have time. We'll see you soon," Liz said. "Maybe you'll remember who bought the last whistle. The one we found looked kind of new."

She turned, knocking over a fish food stand. "Come on, Jake." She pushed him by the shoulder and stumbled out.

"Come back anytime," Mr. Goodman called after them. "And don't forget to go see Stanley. He's all alone to-day."

"Who wants to see creepy Stanley?" Jake mumbled as they went out the door.

"What's wrong with Stanley?" Liz asked.

"He's creepy. He's in my class and I know." Jake

slapped his baseball cap on the side of his leg, then plunked it back on his head.

"What's he done to you?" Liz asked.

"He doesn't talk to me. He doesn't even have a dog, and his father's got that shop," Jake said with disgust.

"Maybe he thinks you're creepy, too. Maybe that's why he doesn't talk to you."

As Jake stopped to face her, Liz held up her hand. "Peace! We've got more important things to do than fight. I thought maybe the last whistle sold would be a clue. We'll come back later. Maybe Mr. Goodman will remember something."

They had walked in the direction of home without thinking about it. As they neared Sam's house, Liz stopped. "Maybe we should go back to the ransom note. It might give us a lead."

They climbed the front steps this time and opened the door. "Sam," Liz called. "It's us again."

"Come on up." *Thump!* "No call, yet." *Thump* came the sound of crashing clay.

"Can we see the ransom note?" Liz yelled.

"Sure, it's in the kitchen on the bulletin board, but don't handle it too much," she called down.

Liz and Jake saw it right away. Sam had taken everything else off the board. There it was, stark, alone, pinned right in the middle of the cork.

I HAVE YOUR DOG
YOU CAN GET HER BACK SOON
NO POLICE MEN

The note was written in big, purple Magic Marker on a torn piece of paper.

"That's funny," said Liz.

"What's so funny about it? You sure find funny things funny," he said.

"I don't mean funny ha ha, silly." Liz reached up and unpinned the note. "Whoever wrote this didn't know policemen is one word."

"Yeah, but it's spelled right . . . isn't it?" Jake asked.

"Yes, in the letters, but that's still not right." She turned the note over and there were two words printed on the back—RECEIVE and RECIPE—but these were in pencil.

"That's spelled right," said Jake proudly. "I know 'cause I spelled 'receive' wrong on our spelling test yesterday."

Liz looked at him with surprise. "Was 'recipe' on your test, too?" she asked.

"Sure, but I got that right," Jake answered.

"You ninny, this is really a clue. It must be someone in your class that took Nelly!"

"How do you figure that?" asked Jake scornfully.

"Part of your spelling test is here on the other side of the ransom note."

"Who'd do anything like that? Why would any of the kids take her?" Jake asked.

"I don't know," Liz answered thoughtfully and chewed on her lower lip.

"What'll we do, go to each kid's house to see if they have Nelly?"

"No, first we'll see if we can track down this purple pen. Come on!"

Liz carefully pinned the note back on the board and started for the front door. Jake hesitated just long enough to grab a handful of Fig Newtons from the cookie jar.

"We'll have to get into school and into your room." Liz was stretching her long legs in a fast walk so that Jake had to jog to keep up.

"We're not allowed in the school on Saturdays," he panted.

"I know that," Liz answered, "but this is an emergency."

The school yard was empty as they approached the fence. The windows of the building were filled with cutouts and art work. You could almost tell which grade was in each room from the outside looking in. The kindergarten had bunnies pasted all along the glass, getting ready for Easter.

"I'm sure the front doors are locked," said Liz. "Let's go around to the back parking lot and see if the teacher's door is open." She hopped over the chain that was strung across the driveway and headed quickly for the back entrance.

"It's open. How did you know?" asked Jake as he tried the handle.

"When you've been in the same school for six years, you know it pretty well," said Liz. "We came in this way once last December to practice for the Christmas play. Now be quiet. We'll be in trouble if we're caught."

The usually noisy, cheerful hall was suddenly eery. Liz's clogs echoed through the corridors with her first steps. She quickly slid out of them and tucked them under her arm. But even Jake's blue jeans rubbing together seemed to scream through the empty halls.

"Shhh," said Liz as she grabbed the bangle bracelets on her wrist.

They stopped and looked up and down both ways when they got to the bottom of the stairs. They had to reach the second floor to get to the fourth-grade classroom.

"Someone must be here," whispered Liz, "or the door wouldn't have been open."

"Maybe it's old Grave Yard," said Jake quietly. "He's probably cleaning."

"Let's go," said Liz, and she inched her way cautiously up the stairs. She stopped again at the top and looked and listened for any sound. The school was so quiet they could hear their own breathing.

She motioned to Jake and they both crept down the hall, pressed against the wall. The door to the classroom was ajar, but Liz had to push it open more to get inside. The creak of the hinge made them both gasp. She pulled Jake in after her and shut the door behind her.

They both stopped and listened. Liz could almost hear a burglar alarm in her head. After a minute she let out a big sigh. "We made it."

She put her clogs down and walked to the back of the room. "You start with the desks up front, and I'll begin back here," she said in a hushed voice.

"That's my desk, dopey, and I didn't take Nelly!"

"Shh," Liz warned. She turned to the desk in front.

"What are we looking for?" asked Jake uncertainly.

"A purple Magic Marker or any other clue we can find. Just look." Liz was thinking about what would happen if they were caught.

In several desks she found the spelling test for Friday and different kinds and colors of pencils. But no purple one.

"Hey, Betty Jo got a hundred on her spelling test," Jake cried.

"Jake, tend to business," Liz said. She had almost covered the back desks, and she and Jake were about to meet in the middle of the classroom.

"It's here!" yelled Jake. "I found it."

"Shh." Liz grabbed the purple marker out of his hand.

"It's creepy Stanley," Jake said. "I should've known. He's always drawing pictures and making signs for the teacher."

"And WHAT do you two think you're doing?"

Mr. Graves, the custodian, was standing in the doorway, swinging his giant bunch of keys. His stern face and dark coveralls had earned him the name of "Grave Yard" among the kids.

"You're not even in your own desk, Jake." His voice thundered through the empty classroom.

"It's my fault, Mr. Graves," said Liz quickly. "It was all my idea, and we really were trying to help our Aunt Sam."

"By going through other people's property?" He advanced into the room and had Jake by the arm. "I'm surprised at you two!"

"Please, Mr. Graves, let me explain." Liz was close to tears and her hand was shaking as she held up the big purple pen. There was silence as Mr. Graves sat down on the top of a desk.

"Well, I'm waiting," he said coldly.

Liz's words tumbled out once she finally started. She

told him everything that had happened that morning.

"So you see, it must be Stanley Goodman who took our Nelly," she finished. "He could have taken the whistle from his father's shop. The ransom note was on the back of his spelling paper and he's got a purple Magic Marker."

"How do you know it was his paper?" asked Mr. Graves, frowning.

"It must be," said Liz, "and he's the only one with the purple pen!"

"But why would he take a dog when his father owns the pet shop?" asked Jake. "I think Stanley's creepy, but I still don't get it."

"We'll let the police answer that." Liz flounced her long hair back and pushed her glasses up on her nose.

"Now wait a minute," said Mr. Graves. "You haven't any real proof. You're just suspicious. Also, this ransom note you tell me about didn't really ask for any ransom."

"No, but it said he had Nelly!" cried Liz.

"It said someone had Nelly," corrected Mr. Graves. "I think the next step is to go see Stanley and give him a chance to explain."

"Okay," said Liz. "When we find Nelly there, it'll prove he's the kidnapper."

"I'll let you two go on one condition," said Mr. Graves. "You go talk to Stanley." His voice was firm and his tone

final. "And I will have to report this to the principal on Monday."

Liz and Jake hung their heads. "I understand," said Liz. "Don't worry, Jake. I'll take all the blame."

"You go see Stanley." Mr. Graves got up from the desk. "And let me know what happens, you hear?"

Stanley lived in the opposite direction from the school than Liz and Jake. As Liz clomped along, Jake darted about at her side. He always seemed to have more energy than the rest of the family put together. They made their plans as they walked.

"Have you ever been to Stanley's?" asked Liz.

"Are you kidding?" Jake sneered. "I do know where he lives, though. We had to drop him off once after our class trip to the dairy."

"All right, we'll look around outside first," said Liz.

They turned the corner, and there was the Goodman house, half-way into the block. It was an old house with a big porch stretching all across the front. The whole place was neat. The spring flowers lined both sides of the driveway.

"You'd never think a kid lived here," said Jake.

"At least not a messy one like you," Liz laughed, remembering their backyard, cluttered with bicycles and skateboards.

"There's a garage we'd better check out, too," said Jake, ignoring her remark.

The garage door stood ajar, but not even a window was open in the house. It was all silent.

"Do you suppose he's here?" asked Jake.

"That's what his father said, remember? Come on," Liz said as she darted along the side of the driveway. She crouched behind the lilac hedge and made her way toward the garage door.

"Quick, let's make a run for it," Jake whispered. And Liz had to stoop and take off her clogs again.

There was a high window on the back of the garage. Sunlight came pouring down on them as they slid inside the door. A smaller door led off the back to a shedlike room.

"Let's see what's in there," said Liz in a shaky voice. Now that she was really breaking into someone's property, she felt uneasy. School was different. It didn't really belong to one person.

Jake found he was holding Liz's arm, and he suddenly snatched his hand back. "Do you want me to look ... first?" he asked.

"We'll look together," Liz said firmly. The door squeaked as they pushed it open, and they both stopped breathing. The room was small and dark. There were rakes and snow shovels hung neatly around the walls.

"It's just a storage place," said Liz with a deep sigh. They crept on into the room. Only the light from the garage seeped into the room. There were no windows, and the shed was damp and musty. Jake went ahead of Liz, peering into the gloom.

"Look at this fancy bike," said Jake poking into the corner. "Liz, look!" Jake pointed at the floor.

Liz scrambled over the boxes and looked behind the bicycle. As her eyes became accustomed to the dark, she could see a folded blanket covering the inside of a paper carton.

"So what?" she asked. "It's an old blanket."

"It's a dog's bed, or it could be. It is. Look." Jake bent over the box and held up a dog biscuit triumphantly.

"Wow!" Liz took the dog biscuit. "It sure as heck is. Come on. Let's find that Stanley."

As she stumbled back toward the door, it suddenly slammed shut. The shed was dark except for a bit of light coming through the cracks in the boards. She felt for the knob, sliding her fingers over the door frame. "Darn it," she mumbled. "I can't see in here at all now and I don't want to lose my clogs. You'll have to find the knob, Jake."

He peered closely at the door and ran his hand over the edge, then suddenly threw himself against it.

"What are you doing?" cried Liz.

"There isn't any knob on this side. We're trapped!"

"Oh!" said Liz. "Why did it have to bang shut?"

"Maybe it didn't," whispered Jake. "Maybe someone closed it on us on purpose."

Liz let her breath out sharply. She sank to the floor and dropped her clogs. "Stanley? Do you really think he'd lock us in here?"

"If he stole Nelly, he'd do anything, wouldn't he?"

"We've got to get out of here," said Liz. She stood up next to Jake. "Come on, let's push at the door together."

She heaved her shoulder at the door, and the jolt was

just enough. Her glasses slid right down her perspiring face and clattered to the floor.

"Darn! Now I'm really blind," she cried. She dropped to her knees and began running her hands along the floor boards.

"What happened?" asked Jake. He stepped backward and there was a crunch of glass.

"My glasses," yelled Liz. "Oh, no! Now they're broken."

"I'm sorry," said Jake quietly. "I really am."

"I know," said Liz with a sob. "It's my fault. It's just that I feel so helpless without them." She held the broken glasses in her hand and then shoved them into her back pocket.

"What do we do now?" she wondered aloud.

"We could yell for help," said Jake.

"Who'd hear us in this closed-up place? It's even getting hard to breath," she said with a gasp.

"If Stanley did shut us in, he's probably making a getaway with Nelly right now," said Jake angrily. "Come on. We've got to try again on the door."

"Okay," Liz said as she stood up, running her hands up the walls for support. "Are you ready? We'll go on three. One, two, three ..."

The rickety door groaned and gave way. Liz and Jake fell forward into the garage, sprawling on their sides.

Liz looked around and squinted through the haze. "Shh," she mumbled. "Look around. Is there anyone here?"

"No, not a soul in sight," he answered. He looked at the door to the shed. "I can't really tell if we were shut in or not. It could have been the wind through the garage door."

Liz reached back into the room and grabbed her shoes. "Let's go, but you'll have to lead. I can't see that far ahead."

"Come on. No more sneaking around. We've got evidence, remember. Follow me," Jake said as he headed for the house.

"Stanley," he yelled. "Stanley Goodman."

Liz slipped on her clogs and followed right behind him.

"Stanley," she yelled as she beat her fist on the door. "Stanley, you come out here. We know you're in there."

Suddenly they heard it. Nelly's bark. It had to be Nelly. Sam always said she loved everything about Nelly but her shrill yap, which sounded like a screaming pig.

"Stanley! Hey you!" Jake was banging, too, and looked as if he were about to smash another door down.

"You give us Nelly," cried Liz.

"Okay, cut it out." The door swung open and there was Nelly. Her tail was beating against Stanley's arm, and she was yapping with excitement.

Stanley held the little black poodle closely and looked defiantly at Liz and Jake. He did not look like a criminal at all. His thin arms were wrapped around Nelly, and one hand held a dog biscuit. Soft, blond, straight hair rimmed a pleasant, round face.

"It's all your fault," he said and pushed through them and out onto the porch.

"What do you mean?" spluttered Liz.

"Give me that dog," cried Jake. "What do you think you're doing, hurting our Nelly?" He started to grab the dog and Stanley stepped aside and Jake crashed into the railing.

"Hurting her? Are your crazy? You're a creep. I wouldn't hurt an animal for anything." Stanley pushed his glasses up on his nose with one hand and held even more tightly to Nelly with the other one.

"You kidnapped her!" hollered Liz.

"I borrowed her," shouted Stanley.

"You're a creep," yelled Jake.

"Now wait a minute," said Liz more calmly. "You have Nelly. Nelly does not belong to you. She belongs to Sam. That's kidnapping in my book!"

"I borrowed her," shouted Stanley again. "She's a poodle, and I was trying to prove something."

"Prove that she's a poodle?" Jake snapped. "That's really dumb."

"Not that she's a poodle. That I don't get asthma from her."

"Asthma? What's that?" Jake started to reach for Nelly again, and Stanley backed up, protecting the dog.

"I know what it is," said Liz. "You can't breathe. It's some kind of allergy, isn't it?"

"Yes," said Stanley. "Would you believe I'm allergic to dogs? Me, with a father that owns the town pet shop?"

"But why take Nelly?" asked Liz.

"I read in a book that poodles are different 'cause they don't shed hair. That's why their hair gets cut just like ours. It said that people who were allergic to dogs could sometimes have poodles for that reason."

"I still don't see why you had to steal Nelly," said Jake.

"Borrow!" said Stanley.

"But why didn't your father get you a poodle?" asked Liz.

"My mother was afraid," replied Stanley. "I asked the doctor about it, and he said it didn't always work."

"But why not try?" asked Liz.

"Oh, my dad would have," said Stanley. "It's my mom. She gets so scared when I have an attack. She said, 'Why take the chance?' and my dad wouldn't go against her. That's why I *borrowed* Nelly. My mom went to visit my grandmother. This was my chance to keep Nelly around me for a couple of days. Then I could prove it was okay for me to get a poodle."

"Then your father knows you've got Nelly?" asked Liz.

"No, I had her in my room last night. I was going to return her tonight after I showed my dad that she'd been here for a whole day and I didn't have one wheeze."

"What's a wheeze?" asked Jake.

"That's what I sound like when I get asthma. My throat clogs up."

"Is that why you don't play baseball and stuff?" asked Jake.

"Yes," answered Stanley quietly. "I sometimes can't breathe when I run a lot." He stood holding Nelly and rubbing his cheek on her black fuzzy head. "I didn't hurt her, honest. I made a bed for her, and she had dinner and biscuits and everything."

"What's the bed doing in the garage then?" asked Jake.

"I just had her out there this morning so my father wouldn't see her before he left. I wanted the test to be for a whole day."

"You have Sam out of her mind worrying," said Liz.

"I dropped off a note saying Nelly was okay," said Stanley.

"Your note was a ransom note," yelled Jake. "It didn't say she was okay!"

"It wasn't," snapped Stanley. "It said she'd be back soon."

Liz thought back to the note and sighed.

"But Sam thought you had kidnapped her for ransom," said Liz impatiently.

"I'm sorry about that. I really didn't want your aunt to worry about Nelly."

"Okay, the first thing we do is call Sam." Liz advanced on Stanley.

"But my father . . ." stammered Stanley.

"The next thing we do," continued Liz, "is worry about convincing your father. By the way, how's your asthma?"

"None at all," said Stanley with a grin.

The call was made, and after hearing that Nelly was safe, Sam soon calmed down.

"I'll bring her right home, and I really am sorry you worried," Stanley told her.

"What about my father?" he turned to Liz and Jake as he hung up the phone.

"We'll go see him with you, but I've got to get home and get my spare glasses."

"What happened to them?" asked Stanley.

"That reminds me. Did you shut us into the shed?" She squinted and pushed her face up close to Stanley's.

"Are you nuts? I tried to stay away from you when I saw you sneaking around the garage. I knew Nelly would bark if she saw you."

"Well, I guess it was the wind," sighed Liz, "and is Mom going to be mad when she finds out I've broken another pair of glasses."

"As a matter of fact, we broke your door to the shed, but just a little bit," said Jake quietly.

"There was no knob on the inside, and we had to throw ourselves at the door. That's when my glasses slid off." Liz held the pieces of broken lens in her hand.

"Don't worry about the door," Stanley said. "I can fix it. At least I'm good at something. Just as long as your aunt's not mad at me."

"She'll understand when we explain. She's kind of super that way. Come on. It's time to reappear, Nelly."

Stanley carried Nelly all the way to Sam's, since he had given no thought to a leash. Liz and Jake offered to take her, but Stanley wouldn't give her up.

Sam was waiting on the front stoop and flew down the street like a teenager when they came into sight.

"Why didn't you just come and play with her if you wanted?" asked Sam when they were all settled on the front steps. "Anyway, I'm surprised your father, of all people, wouldn't buy you a dog of your own."

"That's just it," began Stanley. "It's not my father. You don't know my mother! She worries about me all the time." He sighed deeply as he scratched Nelly under the chin.

As the whole story came out, Sam completely forgave Stanley for his dog-napping. After scolding him for her

worry, she said, "What we've got to do is convince your mother it's safe. I've heard this about poodles, but sometimes it doesn't work, and your mother just can't stand seeing you sick and hurt, probably."

"But it's worth a try," pleaded Stanley.

"You bet it is," Sam said as she hopped up. "Let's go see your dad."

"No, let us do it alone," said Liz. "We'll take Nelly with us, so he can see that Stanley's had her with him all night and so far he's okay."

"Yeah, come on, Stanley. We're all in this together, I guess." Jake shook his cap out and put it back on, ready for action.

"I'll run in for my glasses and catch up," Liz called as she darted across the lawn.

"How'd you guys ever find Nelly?" asked Stanley while they walked toward the store.

Liz told him about the clues pointing to him. First the whistle, which he could have taken, and then the spelling paper and finally the purple pen.

"What'd you need the whistle for?" Jake asked. "Nelly wouldn't know enough to come when you used it."

"Yes, she did," said Stanley. "I blew it at the outside of your aunt's fence, and Nelly was so curious she trotted to the fence and then ran along it to that hole she'd dug. I followed her and must have dropped the whistle pulling her through."

The store was locked when they got there.

"Why would Pop close up at this hour?" wondered Stanley. "He's usually open all day and just eats a sandwich here in the store for lunch."

They knocked on the window and peered into the darkened shop. Mr. Goodman came from the back with his coat over his arm.

"Stanley, where have you been? I just tried to call you. Nelly! You *have* got Nelly!"

"How did you know?" all three asked at once.

"Mr. Graves called me from the school. He said he thought you might be in trouble and asked if you would have any reason to take Nelly."

"My only trouble now is I want a dog and you won't believe I can have one," answered Stanley.

"You'll see," said Mr. Goodman. "You'll be all choked up in a minute."

"But that's it," said Stanley. "Nelly slept in my room all last night and I'm not sick."

"You've had her all night?" gasped Mr. Goodman. "But that's a crime!"

"I'm sorry I didn't tell their Aunt Sam, but she understands now. I've explained it all to her."

Just then the phone rang and Mr. Goodman turned to answer it. It only took a second before they all realized it was Sam on the other end. Mr. Goodman had a hard time getting in one word.

Finally he hung up and turned to the group. "She's a stubborn lady, that aunt of yours. Okay, she says Nelly can spend the rest of the weekend with you. If you're still all right by Monday, you get a dog of your own. Even your mother will have to give in."

"Poodles aren't dogs," said Liz happily. "They're non-allergic, furry people."

"You may be out of trouble," said Jake sadly. "We're the ones who are going to get it on Monday."

"What do you mean?" asked Stanley.

Liz looked at Jake quickly. "Oh, the principal. I forgot." She leaned against the counter and frowned.

"Grave Yard will be sure to tell the principal on us," said Jake, shaking his head sadly.

"About what?" asked Stanley, looking puzzled.

"Breaking into the school. He caught us," answered Jake.

Mr. Goodman looked from one to the other. "Mr. Graves told me about that," he said. "Of course, it was wrong, but then so was taking Nelly."

"I'll come with you," said Stanley quickly. "It's just as much my fault for starting all this."

"Maybe we could all go," said Mr. Goodman, with a smile. "If you three and your Aunt Sam and I all go to your defense, maybe he'll at least understand why you disobeyed the rules."

"Well, at least we won't face our sentence alone," said

Liz, as she grinned at Jake.

Stanley hugged Nelly closer and drew a deep, clear breath.

"Come on, let's all go eat lunch on Sam," said Liz. "Anyway, Nelly has to pack her weekend bag of toys."